This edition published in Great Britain in MMXVIII
by Scribblers, an imprint of
The Salariya Book Company Ltd
25 Marlborough Place,
Brighton BN1 1UB

© Éditions Mijade MMXIII
Text © Catherine Metzmeyer MMXIII
Illustrations © Grégoire Mabire MMXIII
English language © The Salariya Book Company Ltd MMXVIII

HB ISBN-13: 978-1-912233-76-2

1 3 5 7 9 8 6 4 2

A CIP catalogue record for this book is
available from the British Library.

Printed and bound in Belgium

Printed on paper from sustainable sources

Visit
www.salariya.com
for our online catalogue and
free fun stuff.

Catherine Metzmeyer trained as a teacher before becoming a full-time writer of children's books.

Grégoire Mabire trained as an illustrator at the St Luc Institute in Brussels and is now a full-time illustrator of comics and books for children.

THE STREET CAT GANG

Written by
Catherine Metzmeyer

Illustrated by
Grégoire Mabire

It was afternoon in the great, big city
and the traffic hummed and roared...

except behind the graffitied wall
where the street cats snoozed and snored.

Big Red, Ramses, Piano, Liquorice, Mosquito and Rascal are the street cat gang... and this is their home.

But who is this tiny, curled-up kitty who's napping all alone?

Big Red is the boss cat the others follow.
He yawns and says 'Let's go get something to eat.'

But he tells the little kitty to stay where he is.
'You're too small - you'll just get under
our feet.'

The little kitty feels like crying,
but he decides he will NOT
stay at home.

'I'm going on an adventure, too,
whether the gang likes it or not,
I'm NOT staying here all alone.'

'I have to be brave on this adventure,
even though I'm feeling scared.
And I need a plan
so I'm not found out
- I've got to be prepared!'

'I'll follow the cats from a distance
just like a game of hide and seek.

I'll hop and jump between
rooftops and cars

so they don't spot me –
not one peek!'

So little kitty bounced
along trundling trams...

and skipped from
boat to boat...

and escaped the jaws of a big, barking dog...

and followed the cats... like a ghost!

The street cat gang found a restaurant
and Rascal meowed to raise the alarm.
'C'mon, guys, a bin full of leftovers –
let's tuck in, some are even still warm!'

'Yum!' said Liquorice, licking his whiskers,
'this is much better than a rotten, old rat!'
'I couldn't agree more,' Rascal mumbled
through mouthfuls of mush –
he was a very greedy cat.

And the cats were so busy filling their bellies
that they didn't notice the kitty looking on.
He watched from the shadows
with his stomach growling,
like it was singing a hungry song.

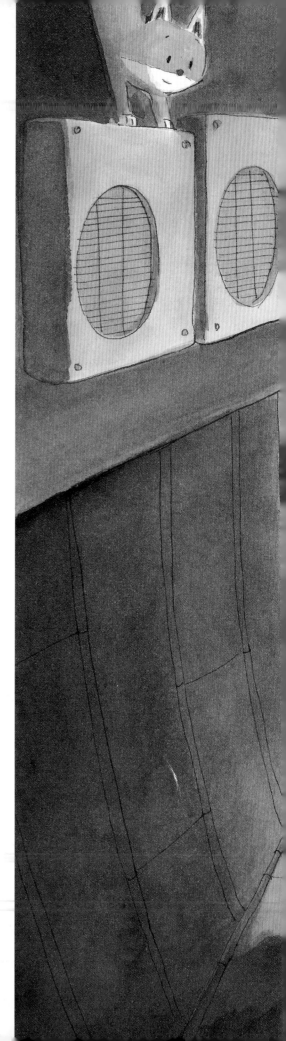

Smoked ham, jelly and yoghurt,
chocolate mixed with lumps of fish –
the bin was filled to the brim with leftovers
that made a strange, mouth-watering dish.

The cats were still so busy filling their bellies
they didn't notice when the wind began,
until a big gust caught the lid of the bin
and crashed down with an almighty

BANG!

'Help! We're trapped!' Piano squeaked,
'oh, what are we to do?'
And the other cats whimpered in the dark of the bin -
not one of them had a clue.

Only the skinny, little kitten was safe
whilst the other cats howled in fear.
'I've got to save them,' Kitty thought,
'and I think I've got an idea...'

The kitty had spied the restaurant's chef and decided to give him a surprise.

He danced, stuck his tongue out
and made mischief.
The chef could hardly
believe his eyes.

The kitty jumped through the open window
and made a horrible mess inside.

'Meow, meow, you can't catch me!'

'Don't be so sure!' the angry chef replied.

'Ha! I can hear you inside my bin,'
the furious chef roared,
'so now I'll make you pay!'

But when he threw open the bin lid
all the street cat gang burst out
and the terrified chef ran away.

'Hooray! We're free!' the street cats cheered.
'Little kitty you saved us!' they sang.

And on that day they named him 'Super Kitty'

and he became a part of the gang.

The End